This book is due for return on

1 3 JUL 2010

2 8 OCT 2015

1 4 OCT 2010

1 2 DEC 2011

0 9 MAY 2012

the light. There was the bright wink of steel
in the candlelight. The moon went out.

The Bishop David Brown School

Look out for other exciting stories
in the *Shades* series:

A Murder of Crows by Penny Bates
Blitz by David Orme
Gateway to Hell by John Banks
Hunter's Moon by John Townsend
Nightmare Park by Phil Preece
Plague by David Orme
Space Explorers by David Johnson
Tears of a Friend by Joanna Kenrick
Who Cares? by Helen Bird

Treachery by Night

Ann Ruffell

Evans

Published by Evans Brothers Limited
2A Portman Mansions
Chiltern St
London W1U 6NR

Reprinted 2007

All rights reserved. No part of this publication
may be reproduced, stored in a retrieval system
or transmitted in any form, or by any means,
electronic, mechanical, photocopying, recording
or otherwise, without the prior permission of
Evans Brothers Limited.

British Library Cataloguing in Publication Data
Ruffell, Ann
Treachery by night. - (Shades)
1. Young adult fiction
I. Title
823. 9'14 [J]

ISBN 978 0 237 52728 0

Series Editor: David Orme
Editor: Julia Moffatt
Designer: Rob Walster

© Evans Brothers Limited 2004

Chapter One

It was the first of May. Conn Macdonald stood halfway up the steep hill and hated his cousin.

The first of May meant the beginning of summer, and plenty to eat. It meant songs outside the straw-thatched houses as you worked during the long days. It meant stories inside the houses during the long, light evenings. It meant driving the last few winter-starved cattle up to the high pastures above Glencoe.

And it meant that Conn Macdonald felt even more left out than usual.

He could hear shouts and yells of triumph away down the slopes of the Black Hill. There was no way he could block out the sound. His keen eyes could see the glint of sun on polished steel, the ant-sized people. And his fifteen-year-old cousin Jamie, teaching the young boys of the glen to be warriors. His own cousin, the same age as himself.

On his ninth birthday Conn had joined his cousin Jamie and the rest of the boys who wanted to learn military skills. They would be taken to a field at the far end of the glen and taught how to use swords and muskets.

He had been so excited he could not eat his breakfast bannock. He had not understood his father's warning not to look forward to something too much.

The grown-ups were kind to him. But it took them a long time to convince him you can't learn the art of fighting with a deformed arm. You can't hold a sword with crippled fingers. That was what they told him on his ninth birthday.

'You have strong legs instead,' his father Alasdair had comforted. 'We need good cattle drivers to take the steers to the best pastures.'

Mairi, his mother, had said nothing, but he could see the pain in her eyes. And he hated her for giving birth to him. What good was it to have strong legs when you couldn't be a man?

And now, six years later, his cousin was

man enough to train the new crop of nine-year-olds to shoot the English. No wonder Conn's heart was full of bitterness.

Then suddenly, in the last week of May, he found something which changed his life for ever.

At the end of the day most people walked down from the high crags, leaving the cattle to browse on the summer grass. But there were shelters for those who guarded their stock against raiders. Conn had taken to staying up on the high pastures with his father's sheep and his uncle's cattle. Down there would be evening tales of great fights against the English and even greater fights against the other clans. These were the last things he wanted to hear.

Until he found the sword.

It was an old broadsword, rusty from

years under the heather. But when he rubbed the blade against a stone, that part of its edge became sharp as a razor. Despite its size, it was beautifully balanced. He could lift it even with his crippled arm.

Was it a sword left by a raider? Or had his clan hidden it with others so that their worst enemies, the Campbells, couldn't find them?

He searched for several days, but found no other weapons. It didn't matter where it had come from. He loved it. Each day he rubbed at the rust with heather stems and sharpened more of its edge.

Nobody had ever suggested he could hold a sword in his left hand. Nobody saw how comfortable it was there. Nobody saw how easily he could brandish the great weight above his head.

His first instinct was to rush down the

mountainside and show his father. But something held him back. They had laughed at him when he was a child, wanting to be a Highland warrior. They would laugh again, that he would even think he could use it. They might admire the way he had cleaned and sharpened it, then they would take it away and give it to someone else.

From hidden crevices of the mountains he began to watch Jamie's military 'school'. Each morning his cousin took the young boys through their movements down on the lower meadows. Some days they learned to aim with muskets. If he was pleased with them, Jamie would fill the barrels with powder and the sharp reports would echo round the hills. But on other days they practised cuts and parries with wooden sticks. Now Conn's sharp eyes watched with professional interest.

Each evening he walked back to the concealed corries and practised the moves he had seen. But he did not practise with sticks. He had his own sword. It began to feel like part of himself. His good arm, he was pleased to note, was becoming as strong as his legs. And now, when he made his rare trips back to the township and his home, he would be able to listen to the tales and imagine himself as hero.

'I'll show them I'm as good as them,' he yelled to the darkening mountain. The steer beside him bellowed.

Deliberately, carefully, Conn thrust the sword at the beast's skin. The wicked point sliced through the beast's hide, right into the vein by the neck. The animal flinched as though attacked by a horse fly. Blood welled and dripped.

With his teeth set in a grin, Conn dropped the sword. It clanged on stone. With his good hand he grabbed the animal by the horns and forced it to stand still.

Then he bent his head and licked the blood from the beast's side. It tasted sharply of metal.

'With this blood I shall be a warrior!' he vowed.

Chapter Two

That year the sun shone cloudless on the fertile fields. Early mists on the high crags had dried out by mid-morning. Oats and barley grew pale and dropped their hard, thin kernels on to baked earth. Rain, in this rainy country, did not come. Conn walked tirelessly to find new green plants for his cattle. But the tufts of grass were few, and those mostly dried out.

There would be nothing to spare for winter fodder. There was barely enough to spare for their own winter needs. Summers were always fat and winters lean, but next winter would be leaner than usual. There were fewer cattle to take down the glen to the markets. What were left were already too thin to live over a winter. Mairi wore a new line across her forehead. But Alasdair simply laughed and said there were ways of getting by.

The trouble was that little of the land in Glencoe belonged to any of them outright. Most people said it was because of crooked laws. If, long ago, the Macdonalds lost the right to own the land in their own glen it was because the Campbells knew how to twist the Law. They were harder-headed and less poetic than the Macdonalds. And though the Macdonalds kept their right to live and farm on the land, a rent had to be paid to the Campbells at Argyll.

Rain came at last, but too late to save crops or animals. The Macdonalds needed cattle, so they would take cattle. They were raiders by profession. And who better to take by surprise than the Campbells of Argyll?

The raid began after dark.

Conn tried to control his shaking body as he crouched against the drenched rock of the hillside. He was not cold, nor afraid of being discovered by the Campbells.

He was afraid of being discovered by his family.

'No, Conn. If there was any trouble you wouldn't be able to defend yourself,' his father had said. 'If we had to come to your rescue we'd all be done for.'

Conn's eyes strained through the darkness, to the powerful sides of the hills around him. They looked as though they could easily walk towards each other and crush the puny bones of a man caught between them. He could almost hear the silence, broken every few seconds by the hush of a foot through the heather or the slap of a hand on to a biting gnat.

They went like ghosts. The chief men rode on their short, dun-coloured horses. Boys and young men walked on foot. In front of them, as if enchanted, streamed the cattle. And behind everyone, Conn dodged unseen.

The Glencoe men knew how to use the animals' natural instinct to draw away from men. They knew how to sting like an insect with their blades to hurry them on. They led the herd away from the Campbell houses, watching for movements which might show that someone had seen. Conn slunk near the houses – surely this grand one belonged to the chief? He ought to move away. He was far too close. But there was another movement, and he froze again.

A stray cow – or was it a stray cow? – danced round a huddle of thatched buildings, and the figure of a man danced after it. Conn could see him now. He was a man who danced with death. Deliberately he goaded the beast round the house of sleeping people. Once, twice, he ran her round, and looked as though he would do it once more. Conn bit his lip and clenched his hands. If the people awoke, there would be blood on the plaids of the Macdonalds before dawn. What did he think he was doing? The night was too fine. There were breaks in the cloud cover. They must all get away quickly.

Then, as the moon suddenly appeared from behind a cloud, Conn recognised the dancing man.

It was his cousin Jamie!

And just as he realised that, a light appeared in a doorway. A shadow blocked the light. There was the bright wink of steel in the candlelight. The moon went out.

Conn stared frantically round in the dark. Panic made his heart beat so that his head was full of the noise of it. It was sheer luck that fear made him stand ice-still. The stolen black cattle were way ahead now. The sound of their hooves was no more than a whisper of a breeze.

The shadow stood still. Conn barely dared breathe in case the mist from his mouth showed up in the cold air.

The figure turned, and the door began to close.

Someone – Conn hoped it was not himself – let a relieved foot slip. One pebble fell on to another pebble.

The door opened again, fast, and more than one person came out of it, shouting to neighbours.

His cousin would have to look after himself. Conn thought he could slip by, and began to creep into the shadows at the back of the house.

Then he saw a horse. And by the horse, Jamie's shadow.

The Campbells held up torches, hastily lit from fires inside the house. The flickering fire gleamed on the coat of the animal. The horse whinnied sharply in fear as the fire came near. Conn saw a blade glitter as the Campbell men searched for thieves.

He was trapped! The Campbells were between himself and freedom.

Feeling for his sword, he rushed into the midst of them. He waved it wildly, all elbows. Then something made him calm down, and remember those lessons he had watched from halfway up the Black Hill.

He parried a thrust and stuck out his foot so that the man stumbled and missed. The horse whinnied and reared. Then Conn grabbed at its mane and hung on, his feet frantically scrabbling at the animal's sides. He hoped desperately that Jamie had already gone, and that he hadn't stolen his cousin's mount.

They were far down the glen before he could haul himself up on to its back.

He heard another horse pound behind him. Yelling at his own horse he turned, ready to protect himself with his sword.

And saw his cousin.

Neither had breath to speak, but Conn saw the glint of Jamie's teeth.

At last they were climbing the Devil's Staircase, the mountain at the top of their own glen. The stolen cattle were flowing in front of the rest of the Macdonald raiding party.

'So whose horse did you steal?'

Conn was confused. He slid off the horse quickly, leading it by the mane towards the party of men who were grinning at him. Who should he give it back to? All the chiefs seemed to be already mounted. Had someone been killed? Then why were they laughing at him?

'I'm sorry,' he said.

'It's a very fine beast,' said Jamie's father, patting the animal on its sweating sides.

Conn's eyes flickered nervously from side to side, searching for anything in their faces which might give him a clue to the horse's ownership.

'And a very nice sword,' said Alasdair.

Conn swallowed.

'The sword's mine. I found it up the hill. A long time ago.'

'Why did you come?' said one of his father's friends. His voice was fierce.

They gathered round him, and Conn backed away.

'Because – because – to help on the cattle raid.'

'But this is not a cow,' pointed out another.

'I—'

But the men could not keep their laughter in any longer. With great guffaws they closed in further and walloped him on the back.

'Instead of cattle, to take the chief's own horse!'

'I what?' He couldn't understand for several moments what they were talking about. It seemed as if, far from doing wrong, he had done something which was right. But what did they mean? The chief's own horse? That belonging to MacIain himself?

But MacIain was already astride his own horse, his legs dangling over the short animal.

'You have brought one of their horses,' grinned Alasdair.

Conn gulped. 'I have? But I thought I was rescuing—'

There was another wild shout of laughter, but then they stopped.

Conn took firm hold on the mane and, walking up to his high chief, presented the horse to MacIain Macdonald.

'It is a gift for you,' he said, looking straight into his chief's wild, proud eyes.

The roar of approval rang and echoed through the hills. Then the raiding party moved again to take the cattle to their final hiding place.

Conn looked round for his cousin. Had Jamie approved of what he had done?

But Jamie Macdonald was already at the front, running fast at the side of his father's horse.

As they moved, the raiding party remembered the dance of the cow round the Campbell house, and complained with admiration.

'That Jamie Macdonald! He'll have us all murdered with his tricks!'

It was a story that would be turned to poetry and told and retold round the fires.

They stowed the animals high in the secret places of the corries on the Black Hill so that they would never be found by a stranger to the glen.

As Conn returned to his home he saw the familiar figure of his cousin, and his heart jumped painfully.

Jamie had come to take a dram of whisky with Conn's father and celebrate their success.

Would he be angry with Conn? He couldn't swear to it, even now, that it was not himself who had kicked the stone that gave them away.

But his cousin stayed at the door, his smile reaching out so far that Conn looked behind him. There was no one else – only the great, towering hills.

'Well done. You're quite a swordsman. Where did you learn?'

'I watched you. From the hill. When you were teaching the young ones.'

Jamie whistled. 'I couldn't have asked for a better pupil. It's a good sword, and you have kept it well. I wouldn't like to be an enemy with you behind it.'

Perhaps it was as well that at that moment his father came out of the warm, smoky house to take Jamie inside for his dram. Conn could not speak. His crippled hand shook. But the good arm clutched at the weight of his sword, as he waited for the stinging water in his eyes to melt in the soft rain.

When he went inside to join the company he wore the sword at his side. With pride.

Jamie gave him lessons now. There were still things to learn. He needed a partner to try to catch him by surprise, to train his reflexes. The best swordsman of the clan came to spar with them both.

'Together you're invincible!' he laughed, only just dodging in time as Conn's left-handed thrust nearly nicked him. 'Anyone who jumps out of Jamie's way will get Conn's broadsword in the neck from the other side!'

He didn't keep the sword up on the hill with the cattle any more. Instead, he spent many of his evening hours polishing it until it glowed bright as moonlight.

'Keep it safe,' his cousin had warned.

He kept it safe. And sharp.

And hidden.

He didn't know how important that was to be.

Chapter Three

It was only a week after the raid that they heard the news.

King William had offered pardon to all the Highlandmen accused of treachery and rebellion.

'Pardon? For what? For our loyalty to King James, our true king?' cried Jamie Macdonald that evening.

There had been no singing on the Black Hill that night, no tale-telling and no piping. The air was full of argument.

'Why should we do what this new king wants?' said Conn.

'Why? Because he is the king,' said peaceful Mairi.

'I could understand if the Campbells had to go and bow their knees,' said Jamie. 'But they're in the new king's pocket.'

The arguments went backwards and forwards, all through the evening and over the next days and nights. But then word came from MacIain himself that he was willing to go and sign the peace treaty. If King James agreed.

But King James was exiled in France, hundreds of miles away. He did give his permission for the chiefs of the Highlands to swear allegiance to the new King William.

But by the time the message came back to Glencoe it was the 29th of December.

Chief MacIain Macdonald had two days before the deadline.

Yet no one was panicking. There was still time. The chief chose his guides and helpers. Jamie was to be one of them.

It was all quite straightforward.

'I don't like the weather,' said Conn's father uneasily. 'It is too good. When it changes, it will change fast.'

Sure enough, as soon as the little party had left, with the chief on his dun-coloured horse and his helpers running alongside, the snow began to fall.

It was the foulest weather Conn had ever known.

The hills disappeared in a fleece of whirling white and the wind piled up great drifts to make new hills. It was a struggle for Conn to hack his way to the byre to feed the cows. Brutal, freezing snow sliced his cheeks and knifed his bare legs. Even the big peat fire in the centre of the room seemed to give out no heat.

There were no gatherings in the evening. People did not want to risk the short walk up a hillside in case the hillside changed shape while they were out.

Besides, no one wanted to sing until MacIain and his helpers returned from Inveraray.

News did come, just before the ending of the old year. One of the helpers – it was not Jamie – struggled the last half mile in violent, white darkness to bring it to the chief's family at Carnoch.

It took Alasdair two hours to walk the few yards in clinging snow to Carnoch, and another two to bring back the news.

'He went to Fort William,' said Alasdair slowly, shaking the fresh snow off his head.

'To *Fort William?*' Mairi spread her hands in amazement. 'But that's the wrong way!'

'It was closer,' snapped Alasdair. 'And the king's officers were there.'

'Then he's signed the paper?'

'It was not possible. They have to go to Inveraray.'

Conn knew they would not be able to go the short way across the hills to Inveraray. Not even a deer could do that in a normal winter. This was not normal. He tried to imagine the terrible walk along the lochside.

He listened to the wind screaming bitterness outside and wondered if they would ever return.

But they did return, though it took them until a week after the New Year. They came in sunshine, which already began to melt snow into the burns. And as the flame of warmth lit the mountain-tops with gold, MacIain ordered a great fire to be lit on top of the rock at the bend of the River Coe, and spoke to them all.

He had taken the oath, not only in his name but on behalf of them all. It was now up to his people to live peacefully under King William.

Conn went with his parents and sisters to Jamie's house a day later to hear the details of their journey.

It had been worse than anyone imagined.

Chapter Four

'He told us we should go to Fort William, to swear before the governor. If we had gone to Inveraray, he would have to swear in front of a Campbell, and you know how he would like that!'

'In front of a Campbell! A Macdonald to bow his knee before a Campbell! And one who's changed his kilt for a red coat!'

Jamie's father was horrified and insulted. The bitter rivalry between these two clans had endured for centuries. It was too long a time even to be healed by the recent marriage between a Campbell and MacIain's son.

Jamie suddenly sniggered.

'How can you laugh at such a thing?'

'I'm not laughing at that. I was laughing at the memory of our last visit to Campbell country!'

Conn grinned, though a little shiver of horror gripped his stomach remembering the narrowness of their escape.

'MacIain was sure Colonel Hill would allow him to swear there instead. It was only a formality. He'd proved he meant to do it.'

'You can't bend English law,' said Mairi sharply. 'We've learned that.'

'We had *not* learned that,' said Jamie, his laughter gone. 'But we didn't know that the Law was so cruel as to make us go back and down to Inveraray in such weather. Even our eyelashes were frozen. He could see that! And how could we have got there in time? In good weather it would have been just possible, over the hills. But in that blizzard! Colonel Hill knew it was impossible.'

There was worse. They had bumped into a patrol of Redcoats, who had thrown them into a dungeon for a day and a night.

'The old year had gone by before we were let out,' said Jamie bitterly. 'And we still had a long way to go.'

As he described the terrible journey his hands shook as if with the cold, though he was close to the fire. They had gone through glens and mountains passes, stumbling through the relentless snowstorms, moving at about a mile an hour. Then at last, on the second of January, they saw the tall castle of Inveraray below them.

'And when you got there?' asked Conn.

'The sheriff was not there,' said Jamie bleakly. 'He was seeing in the New Year with his family, away across the loch. Nobody expected him back until the weather improved.'

'But he shouldn't have gone at such an important time!' shouted Conn.

'If we had arrived in time, he would not,' said Jamie. Then he burst out, 'As it was, we had to wait another three days. Three days in Campbell country! I tell you, I was scared!'

Alasdair patted him on the back of his hand.

'I would have been scared too. There's no shame in that.'

'But the sheriff? What did he say?'

'The chief swore his oath, and the sheriff said he would send the colonel's letter south to Edinburgh with another letter of his own.'

Alasdair stood up, squaring his shoulders.

'Then if we keep our oath, there is nothing to be afraid of.'

Chapter Five

It did seem as if there was nothing to be afraid of as the days grew longer. Life went back to normal. Conn looked forward to Spring and a time when he could impress his cousin with new sword skills.

But at the beginning of February they heard that an army of Redcoats was heading their way.

Worse, at its head was Captain Robert Campbell, one of their ancient enemies.

MacIain laughed. He had signed the oath, hadn't he? There was nothing to worry about. But he did not trust soldiers not to steal a few guns and blades while they were nearby.

'Hide them in the peat stacks and under the rocks of the hillside,' MacIain instructed. 'Let them have only the rusty and blunt ones if they do come thieving.'

The Highlandmen took their polished swords, their oiled muskets, out from their houses and up the dark slopes.

Conn felt no guilt about keeping his own sword hidden in his bed. It had been rusty and blunt, he reasoned. He wasn't doing anything wrong. He didn't know why he felt *someone* needed to have a good weapon around. Maybe it had been the look in Jamie's eye when the news had come. Maybe it was the sudden indrawn breath from his mother.

Maybe it was some sixth sense of his own.

'We come in peace, as friends,' said the captain.

He smiled at MacIain, even though MacIain's men had raided his valley after a battle nearly three years ago.

And MacIain didn't flinch. Instead, he opened his arms.

'Welcome!' he roared. 'Never let it be said that a Macdonald refused to give hospitality to a Highlandman. Where are you bound?'

'North,' said the captain. 'There are still some foolish clans who refused the king's pardon. We need to rest a while and wait for our orders.'

Conn watched MacIain's expression. There seemed no shadow of suspicion on his ruddy face. MacIain obviously believed that his intention to sign before the end of the year was as good as getting there in time. And that the letters, sent to Edinburgh, had been received.

'You shall have meat and drink and a fire to sit by,' said the Glencoe chief generously. 'Each family will take in a soldier. Let us feast and be friends!'

The Glencoe families sighed with relief. If they were to be hosts to the soldiers, there was no possibility they would be attacked.

Besides, the captain's niece was married to MacIain's own son. What could possibly go wrong?

But some of the Glencoe men muttered darkly.

'I don't like it,' said one, called Ranald. 'He has no reason to love us.'

A hundred men went to their chief to point this out, but MacIain, instead of listening to them, rounded on them angrily.

'They are Highland, as we are Highland,' he said. 'The law of hospitality is strong. No harm will come to you, and you should not offend them.'

'I might be offended,' said Ranald, 'if he had taken as many cattle from our glens as we took from his.'

But the community settled down happily enough with the Redcoats – the Highland ones, at least – strange though it seemed to some of them.

But Jamie Macdonald, nodding over to the man by the fire, muttered to his cousin Conn, 'Keep an eye on that one.' Outwardly he grinned at Mairi and

Alasdair's guest, and challenged him aloud to a trial of strength.

Conn joined in the fierce games of shinty during the short afternoons, cracking many a Campbell's shin with his stick and receiving as many bruises back.

'I can't see anything wrong with them,' he said to Jamie one evening.

His cousin's eyes narrowed as he looked at the other group of soldiers. These were the outsiders, the Lowlanders, shivering at the edge of the main company.

'They're not Highlanders,' said Jamie. 'How can we expect them to know our customs? I don't like it, Conn. Why can't they move on?'

'They have to wait for their orders.'

'So we look after them, and play. But I hope they don't play too long. We're running out of stores. If they stay much longer we'll have to go visiting Glenlyon again to fill our storehouses.'

And then the weather changed again.

It was cold, cold, with snow waiting to fall from heavy clouds. Conn played cards with his sisters and his young cousins, and the soldiers from the Argyll regiment played with them. Smoke from the fires whisked about them. Mean nips of cold wind snapped at their ankles.

Alasdair looked at his nephews.

'Boys, you must go home before the storm breaks. Girls – to bed.'

Conn went to the door with his cousins. He watched the boys until they were round the end of their own house, then with one last look turned to go in.

As he turned he saw men. Too many men. Not in warm, companionable groups, but in shifty twos and threes. They were murmuring, then moving away again.

'Father—'

But his parents had their arms round each other for their last look at the fire before bed.

And their guest was no longer there.

Chapter Six

Conn went behind the woollen screen to his own bed. He felt for the familiar broadsword, concealed in the springy heather mattress. The hilt of it felt comforting to his fingers. He heard the door clack, the soldier enter. He heard his father call out the offer of a nightcap. He heard the voices rise and die as the wind shrieked round the mountains.

Then he heard the voices closer to him.

'We have our marching orders.'

It was their guest.

'It is not a good night to march.' His father's voice, sympathetic.

'It is not.'

And that was all. There was no request for a plaid to warm himself. Their guest did not ask for a drink. There was no talk of their route, their plans.

Outside there was a swirling blizzard. What kind of commander would tell his men to move on in this, especially after waiting two weeks?

Conn felt fear grow in him.

As the night slunk on, he could not sleep. He kept hearing sounds outside, rattling of weapons against the scream of the gale.

It could, of course, be the soldiers making ready for their early start. But there was something too stealthy about their movements. You would have expected loud curses, complaints about the weather and the early hour.

Conn slid the sword out of his bedding. Why, why had MacIain told them all to hide their weapons? What good were weapons hidden in the peat bogs? They needed them here, in their hands, at the ready!

The wind howled wildly and in the noise there came another sound. The appalling scream of a woman.

Conn grabbed the plaid from his bed. He clutched his sword in a shaking hand and pushed through the blanket partition.

Their guest, in his red coat, pointed the musket straight at him.

Chapter Seven

Startled, the soldier aimed badly. The musket ball went straight through a window. Conn fell to the floor in shock. The soldier, thinking he had killed the boy, ran out to join his fellows.

'Father!' shouted Conn. It should have been a warning, but it was disaster.

A volley of shots echoed in the glen.

As Conn's father leaped from his bed in his nightgown, another shot from outside killed him in his own doorway.

Sobbing with fear and despair, Conn yelled to his mother and sisters. 'Run! Run out of the back! Run!'

And without waiting to see whether they obeyed him, he flung himself on to his father's body, crying like a baby.

It was minutes before he could move again. Then he was filled with a huge and terrible anger against the men who had taken their food and whisky and cut them down worse than animals.

The sounds of attack grew nearer again. Conn rose and dashed the tears from his eyes. Cold now, in his murderous rage, he stood over his father's body and defended his house.

The glen was full of screams and cries and the sound of musket fire. But the sword in his good hand gave him courage. Again and again he slashed at movements in the dark, sometimes finding flesh. The heavy blade sang in the gale. Muskets barked, but the balls never came near to him. The powder was wet and the soldiers could not see to aim in the snow.

Then his arm grew heavy. He had worked hard on his muscles, but not like the other men of the glen who had been doing it all their lives. The blade began to droop.

Suddenly there was another man at his side. A man with another blade, a coarse and rusted blade.

'Jamie!'

'Keep at it, man!' shouted his cousin. 'Give time for the women and babes to run.

We'll see a few of these traitors to an early grave before we go too.'

Conn saw the flash of his teeth as he wielded his old blade as usefully as Conn thrust his own bright one.

Heat filled him once more. His arms lifted. The next soldier who came at him roared with pain at the frozen steel in his gut.

Side by side they fought, dodging to escape the musket fire. They were blinded by snow, but each time they sliced at a soldier it gave a bit more time for the women and children to escape into the high corries.

Suddenly, Jamie's sword was knocked from him. Conn heard it clang on to the hard rock. Without thinking, he flung his own sword to his cousin. Out of the corner of his eye he saw a soldier take aim.

He ran to push Jamie out of the way.
A musket ball grazed his ear, but Jamie, staggering, was still alive.

'Run, Conn!'

'I can't – I won't!'

'*Run!*'

'I can't *leave* you!'

'*Run!*'

He knew he had to. He was no use now, weaponless.

'Look after the others!'

Wildly he looked around. The soldiers were still advancing terribly towards them. Jamie stood fending them off, Conn's blade glittering in the snowlight.

He had no chance. No chance at all.

Sobbing, despairing, he ran away up the hill into the teeth of the blizzard. If he couldn't help Jamie, at least he could find and protect his mother and sisters.

Below, the soldiers set fire to the roofs of the houses, and flames rose into the frozen air.

Chapter Eight

Bleak morning broke and soldiers still roamed the glen, searching for more Macdonalds to kill. It was not until late afternoon that the last of them had gone.

Then down from the hills came a few brave Macdonalds, still in their nightwear, to find their dead. It was so cold they could barely move, but they needed to salvage what they could from their burned homes.

It was black round the houses and still warm from the fires, but snow covered everything else. Conn searched the humps in the ground, desperate to find his cousin's body before taking a plaid no one needed any more.

He saw the sword first. It lay with only a light covering of snow on it, next to the prone body. Jamie had fallen far enough away from the buildings not to have been burned with them.

Conn knelt in the snow. He touched his cousin, his heart dead within him.

Jamie's eyes fluttered open.

'Jamie!' Conn's joy was so great he could hardly speak. He stuttered. 'Come – I'll take you back to where it's safe. Here – the sword. It's still here.'

Eagerly he picked up his sword and pressed the hilt into his cousin's hand.

With a last effort Jamie pushed it away. But he pushed it in such a way that left Conn in no doubt he was being given it back, as his right. The right of a man who was now a worthy head of his family.

'You're a brave man, Conn Macdonald,' said Jamie, before he died.

Afterword
The Massacre of Glencoe

The story of the massacre at Glencoe is true.

The politics behind the story are complicated, but basically King William wanted to unite England and Scotland. The Highlanders, followers of the exiled King James, were difficult to convince. However, when King William offered to pardon them for long years of rebellion and murder, many of the clans decided to take an oath of allegiance to the English king. The Campbells were among the first to take this oath. Many became soldiers in William's army and wore the uniform red coat.

It wasn't MacIain's fault that he was late getting to Inverary to take his oath. It was partly King James' fault – he dithered for three months before he gave the chiefs permission to go – and partly the dreadful weather. But the commander of William's army, sent to the Highlands to sort out the rebel clans who didn't sign, was a Campbell.

The Macdonalds and the Campbells had always been enemies – mainly because the Macdonalds were efficient cattle-raiders and had stolen even more than cattle from their neighbours.

The Campbell captain was very pleased that technically MacIain had missed the deadline. He was not the only person who hated the wild rebel Macdonalds. The Secretary of State for Scotland, Viscount Stair, was another. His instructions to the captain were to 'put all to the sword under seventy' and to 'be secret and sudden'.

The story is the more terrible because the soldiers who murdered the clanspeople had been guests of the Macdonalds (though some of the soldiers did secretly warn their hosts).

I have invented Jamie and Conn. But certainly there would have been heroes on that dreadful day, brave young men like Jamie and Conn Macdonald.

Blitz - David Orme

It's World War II and Martin has been evacuated to the country. He hates it so much, he runs back home to London. But home isn't where it used to be…

Gateway from Hell - John Banks

Lisa and her friends are determined to stop the new road being built. Especially as it means digging up Mott Hill. Because something ancient lies beneath the hill. Something dangerous - something *deadly*…

A Murder of Crows - Penny Bates

Ben is new to the country, and when he makes friends with a lonely crow, finds himself being bullied. Now the bullies want him to hurt his only friend. But they have reckoned without the power of crow law…

Hunter's Moon - John Townsend

Neil loves working as a gamekeeper. But something very strange is going on in the woods… What is the meaning of the message Neil receives? And why should he beware the Hunter's Moon?

Space Explorers - David Johnson

Sammi and Zak have been stranded on a strange planet, surrounded by deadly spear plants. Luckily mysterious horned-creatures rescue them. Now all they need to do is get back to their ship…

Who Cares? - Helen Bird

Tara hates her life – till she meets Liam, and things start looking up. Only, Liam doesn't approve of Tara taking drugs. But Tara won't listen. She can handle it. Or can she?

Look out for these new Shades titles

Plague - David Orme

The year is 1665 and plague has come to the city of London. For Henry Harper, life will never be the same. His father is dead, and his mother and brother have fled to the country. Now Henry is alone, and must find a way to escape from the city he loves, before he, too, is struck down…

Treachery by Night - Ann Ruffell

Glencoe, 1692
Conn longs to be a brave warrior, just like his cousin Jamie. But what kind of warrior has a withered arm? Then he finds a sword in the heather, and he learns to fight using his good arm. And when the treacherous Campbells bring Redcoats into the Macdonald valley, Conn is going to need all the strength he can muster…

Nightmare Park - Philip Preece

Dreamland… a place where your dreams come true.
Ben thinks it's a joke at first. But he'd give anything to be popular. Losing a few short minutes of his life seems a small price to pay. But a lot can happen in a minute. And Ben soon realises nothing in life should be this easy…

Tears of a Friend - Joanna Kenrick

Cassie and Claire have been friends for ever. Cassie thinks nothing will ever split them apart. But then, the unthinkable happens. They have a row, and now Cassie feels so alone. What can she do to mend a friendship? Or has she lost Claire … for good?